Is the Clue Crew up to the task?

"Are you sure no one suspects what we're doing?" the boy asked.

"I'm sure," Deirdre said.

"What about those three girls you call the Clue Crew?" the boy said.

"Ha!" replied Deirdre. "This mystery is way too hard for them!"

Join the CLUE CREW
& solve these other cases!

NANCY DREW

AND THE CLUE CREW™

#7

The Circus Scare

BY CAROLYN KEENE

ILLUSTRATED BY MACKY PAMINTUAN

Aladdin Paperbacks
New York London Toronto Sydney

ALADDIN PAPERBACKS

An imprint of Simon & Schuster Children's Publishing Division

1230 Avenue of the Americas, New York, NY 10020

Text copyright © 2007 by Simon & Schuster, Inc.

Illustrations copyright © 2007 by Macky Pamintuan

All rights reserved, including the right of reproduction in whole or in part in any form.

ALADDIN PAPERBACKS, NANCY DREW AND THE CLUE CREW, and colophon are trademarks of Simon & Schuster, Inc.

NANCY DREW is a registered trademark of Simon & Schuster, Inc.

Designed by Lisa Vega

The text of this book was set in ITC Stone Informal.

Manufactured in the United States of America

First Aladdin Paperbacks edition April 2007

20 19 18 17 16 15 14 13 12

Library of Congress Control Number 2006939099

ISBN-13: 978-1-4169-3486-8

ISBN-10: 1-4169-3486-3

0315 OFF

CONTENTS

The Circus Scare

CHAPTER ONE

Deirdre's Secret

"There's a parking spot, Hannah!" eight-year-old Nancy Drew shouted. "It's right by the mall entrance."

Hannah Gruen, the Drew family's house-keeper, expertly pulled her car into the space and turned off the engine. "Are you ready to shop till you drop?" she asked.

Nancy giggled.

"Yes!" Bess Marvin and George Fayne shouted from the backseat.

It was Thursday morning. Hannah had driven Nancy, Bess, and George to the River Heights Mall to buy new swimsuits for the summer. Besides being cousins, Bess and

George had been Nancy's two best friends since kindergarten. The three girls went everywhere together.

They were also famous for solving local mysteries. The friends had even started their own detective club, which they called the Clue Crew. Their headquarters were in Nancy's room, and they kept every clue they found in Nancy's desk drawer. George wrote their detective files on Nancy's computer. George knew more about computers than almost anyone else in their third-grade class.

For the next hour the three friends tried on swimsuits in Merkle's Department Store. Finally Nancy chose one in lavender, her favorite color. Bess picked a blue one, and George got a red one.

"I want to look in housewares now," Hannah said. "Your father told me to buy some new everyday dishes."

"Could we sit on the benches out in the mall and wait for you?" Nancy asked.

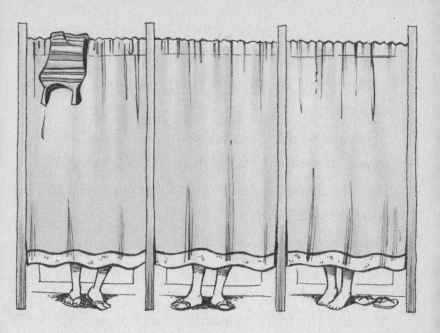

"Please!" Bess said. "I am totally tired from modeling swimsuits!"

Nancy and George rolled their eyes at each other.

"All right," Hannah said, "but stay together."

"We know the rules," the three friends replied.

Just as they left the store, Nancy exclaimed, "Hey, there's a poster for the circus. I can hardly wait until it gets here!"

"Me either!" George said.

"Oh, look! There's Deirdre," Bess said. "Hmm. Why is she going into Feathers and Beads?" Feathers and Beads sold fashion accessories at a discount.

"That's weird," Nancy said. She brushed a strand of reddish blond hair out of her eyes. "Deirdre usually only shops where she can spend a lot of money."

Deirdre Shannon was in the girls' third-grade class. Everyone knew that her parents gave her everything she wanted.

"That's the truth," George said. She sighed. "I could buy a computer for what Deirdre spends on one pair of shoes."

"I smell another mystery here, Clue Crew!" Bess said. "Nancy, get out your purple notebook and pencil and write this all down."

"There's no mystery here, Bess," Nancy said.

"Oh, but there is!" Bess told her. *Why is Deirdre in a store where things don't cost a lot of money?*

"That's easy," Nancy said. "She's already spent her allowance this month."

"But Deirdre doesn't get an allowance," Bess said. "She gets money on demand."

"And she's always *demanding* it," George added with a snicker.

"Well, I guess we could . . . ," Nancy started to say, but just then Hannah came out of Merkle's Department Store. "Girls! I am so excited!" she said. "I found a lasagna dish just like the one we used to have, so I'm going to make vegetable lasagna tonight."

Nancy blushed. "I owe you part of my allowance, then, because when I broke the other one I told you that I'd—"

"No, you don't owe me part of your allowance, dear," Hannah said. She gave Nancy a big hug. "That old dish was chipped in so many places, I had already decided we needed a new one."

Nancy's mother had died when Nancy was three, and Hannah had been taking care of her ever since. Not only was Hannah the best cook, she was also the best hugger, and Nancy knew how lucky she was.

"Thanks, Hannah," Nancy said.

"Are you girls hungry?" said Hannah. "Mr. Drew is treating us to pizza at Pick a Slice here in the mall."

"Oh, I love their pizza!" Nancy said.

"I wasn't hungry until you mentioned Pick a Slice, Hannah," George said. "Now I'm starting to drool."

"Nancy!" said Bess. "Haven't you forgotten something?"

Nancy turned. "What?" she asked.

"*The mystery!*" Bess said.

"What's this?" Hannah said. "A mystery?"

"Bess saw Deirdre in Feathers and Beads and wanted to know why she was there," Nancy explained. "Nothing costs very much there, and we all know how much Deirdre likes to spend money."

"That is a mystery, isn't it?" the housekeeper said.

Bess put her hands on her hips. "See, Nancy!" she said.

"But we're hungry," Nancy and George said.

"Well, Pick a Slice is probably really crowded right now, anyway," Hannah told them, "so I guess it wouldn't hurt to check it out."

"I think we need to make Hannah a member of the Clue Crew," Bess said. "She seems to be the only one besides me who sees a mystery here."

George tossed her dark curls. "We're not going to win this, Nancy," she said with a grin. "We might as well do some sleuthing."

Nancy nodded. "Let's go," she agreed.

The four of them headed across to Feathers and Beads, but when they got inside, Bess cried, "Deirdre's disappeared!"

"She probably left," Nancy said.

"No, she didn't," Bess said. "I was watching the front door the whole time I was talking to you."

"Feathers and Beads is a very small store, Bess," said George. "You can see everything standing in one place."

"She has to be here," Bess insisted. "She did not leave."

"Maybe she went to the restroom," Hannah suggested.

"See! That's another reason Hannah needs to be a member of the Clue Crew," Bess said. "She's sleuthing while you two are thinking about pizza."

"Read that, Bess," said Nancy. She pointed to a small handwritten sign taped to the wall next to a light switch.

"'No Public Restroom,'" Bess read. She shrugged. "That wouldn't stop Deirdre."

"Bess is right, Nancy," George said. "I'll go ask that clerk over there if Deirdre went into the restroom."

"We'll look around the store while you do that, George," Nancy said.

While George talked to the lady behind the counter, Nancy and Bess made their way through the crowded displays of earrings, combs, headbands, and strings of beads.

Suddenly Nancy spotted a familiar pair of sneakers sticking out from the bottom of some long feather boas.

"Well, she's not in the bathroom," George reported, coming up behind them. "The clerk insisted that they don't let customers use it."

"Hi, Deirdre," Nancy said.

George and Bess looked puzzled until Deirdre pulled aside the feather boas and stepped out to face them.

"Nobody was supposed to see me in here, Nancy Drew!" Deirdre hissed angrily. "It's a secret!"

"I told you!" said Bess triumphantly.

ChAPTER TWO

Brownie the Bear

"We know what your secret is," George said.

"What?" Deirdre demanded.

"You're shopping in a store where you don't have to spend a lot of money," Nancy replied.

"And you don't want anyone to find out about it," added Bess.

Deirdre rolled her eyes. "Wrong! And I thought you three were good at solving mysteries," she said. "My secret is that I'm going to have a circus in my backyard this Sunday. And it'll be better than the one that's coming to town too."

"You can't do that, Deirdre!" Bess exclaimed.

"Why not?" asked Deirdre.

"Because our whole class promised to go to every performance of the real circus this weekend, that's why," George said.

"We want to enter all our ticket stubs in the drawing to win the big stuffed Brownie the Bear for the children's hospital," Nancy said.

"But I want to have my own circus!" Deirdre said. "And my parents said I could."

Nancy, Bess, and George glared at her.

Finally Deirdre said, "Okay, okay. I'll tell everybody on my website that they should still go to the *other* circus too."

Deirdre was the only one of their friends who had her own website. She was always writing articles and taking pictures to post on it.

Deirdre smiled. "Everybody at school reads it," she added. "It's like I'm famous, and they all come to me for advice."

"That's scary," George muttered.

Nancy giggled.

"So why are you in Feathers and Beads, then?" Bess asked.

"My mother is making our costumes," Deirdre said. "We're going to wear feathers and beads and sequins, too, just like all the circus performers do."

"Who's 'we'?" Nancy asked.

"So far it's Trina, Ned, Nadine, Marcy, Peter, and Andrea," Deirdre said.

"Why didn't you ask us?" said George.

Nancy was wondering the same thing, since Deirdre had just named several of their friends from school.

"I thought you'd be too busy solving mysteries," Deirdre answered.

"You're right," Nancy shot back. "And we just solved this one, but there are hundreds of others waiting for us, so we'd better be on our way."

Just then Hannah walked up and said, "That was your father on my cell phone, Nancy. The circus train is arriving ahead of schedule. He wants us to meet him at home, and then we can all go to the station to see it. The pizza will have to wait."

Mr. Drew was a busy lawyer, but he was never too busy to do things with Nancy and her friends.

"Do you want to come with us, Deirdre?" Nancy asked. "You might get some ideas for *your* circus."

"I'm supposed to stay here until my mother comes back," Deirdre said. "I'd call her on my cell phone, but it went dead just as we got to the mall."

"That's too bad," Bess said. "Well, good luck with your circus costumes."

Hannah drove them home. Mr. Drew was waiting for them in the driveway.

The railroad station was only a few blocks away, so it didn't take them long to get there. When they arrived, the circus train was just pulling into the station.

Mr. Drew parked the car, and Nancy, Bess, and George leaped out onto the sidewalk.

"Stay together," Hannah shouted to them.

"We know the rules!" Nancy shouted back.

Nancy, George, and Bess all had the same rules. They could walk or ride their bikes five blocks from each of their houses as long as they were together. If they wanted to go anywhere farther away, they had to be driven by either Hannah or a parent.

"Wouldn't it be great if we could solve a circus mystery?" Bess said.

"Who knows?" Nancy said. "We might get lucky."

Just as they passed one of the passenger cars, some circus performers jumped off.

"Wow! Now I know why Deirdre was in Feathers and Beads," Bess said. "These performers are dripping with them."

"They're ready for the circus parade through downtown River Heights," Nancy said. "It's a tradition."

"The animal cars are down this way," said George. "Let's go!"

The girls wound their way through the crowd of people on the platform. For the next several minutes they watched as the circus workers unloaded the elephants, camels, and horses. The lions and tigers stayed in their cages, but they were hitched to horses and carts for the parade.

When Nancy, Bess, and George got back to the car, Mr. Drew and Hannah were standing at the curb.

"This is a good place to see the parade," Hannah said.

Just then a band started playing. Within a few minutes, the band came down the platform and turned onto the street right in front of them.

The band was followed by men and women in colorful costumes. Some were walking. Others were riding elephants, horses, and camels. The clowns were stuffed into tiny automobiles, which couldn't seem to go in straight lines. The clowns were followed by the lions and tigers in cages on wheels, drawn by beautiful horses.

"Look, Nancy," George said. "It's Brownie the Bear!"

Brownie was new to the circus. Everyone was excited because his first performance was in River Heights!

Brownie was walking beside his trainer. Sometimes the bear would stop, stand on two legs, and do a little dance. The crowd would applaud.

Behind Brownie and his trainer was a horse pulling a cage. Inside the cage was the huge stuffed bear that the circus was giving away.

"It looks just like the real Brownie!" cried Bess.

"All the children in the hospital will love that!" Nancy exclaimed.

"They sure will," George agreed.

Just then Brownie stopped dancing. He looked over at Hannah. Suddenly he ran over and grabbed her purse!

Hannah screamed.

"Brownie! Bad bear!" the trainer shouted. "Give the nice lady back her purse!"

Brownie handed the purse back to Hannah. The crowd laughed.

Nancy looked at Bess and George. "I guess

that was just part of his act." She laughed nervously. "But I think we need to keep an eye on that bear. We need to make sure he doesn't take anything else that doesn't belong to him."

CHAPTER THREE

What Happened to the Noses?

Mr. Drew parked the car in a reserved lot not far from the main entrance to the circus tent. It was Friday night and the girls were attending the circus's opening show.

"Look!" Bess shouted. "Elephants!"

"Peanuts! Get your peanuts here!"

"Dad, may we buy some peanuts to feed the elephants?" Nancy asked. "They look kind of hungry to me."

"All right," Mr. Drew said. "We have a few minutes before the circus begins."

Nancy bought three big bags of peanuts from the vendor. Then the three friends ran over to the elephants.

"What are their names?" Nancy asked the elephant trainer.

"Julie, Mary, Fiona, and Nancy," the trainer replied. "Nancy's the hungriest."

Bess and George laughed.

"That's the truth!" Bess said.

The girls put a pile of peanuts in their hands. The elephants used their trunks to pick them up and put them in their mouths.

"That tickles!" Bess said, giggling.

"Why don't they have tusks?" Nancy asked. "I thought all elephants had tusks."

"These are Asian elephants," explained the trainer. "They don't bear tusks like African elephants do."

Just then a band started playing.

"The circus is about to start," Nancy said. "We'd better find our seats so we won't miss the grand entrance."

"Bye, girls!" the three friends shouted to the elephants as they followed Mr. Drew and Hannah into the tent. Their seats were in the fifth row in front of the center ring.

"Hey!" Bess said. She pointed to the other side of the tent. "There's Deirdre." Nancy and George looked. Deirdre was talking to some of the performers as they came into the tent. "I wonder what she's saying."

"She's probably telling them all about her backyard circus," George guessed.

"That would be Deirdre," Nancy agreed.

Just then Deirdre disappeared from their view. "Where's she going? She should be *watching* if she wants to see how a real circus works."

At that moment the band marched by in front of them. Nancy forgot all about Deirdre. The band was followed by the ringmaster, who ran to the center ring. He stood behind a microphone and started announcing the acts as they passed in front of the Clue Crew's section.

First came the jugglers. They were walking on their hands and juggling bowling pins with their feet.

"Do not try this at home!" Bess said.

Nancy and George giggled.

"Here come the clowns!" said Hannah. "I've always loved clowns."

"Really?" Nancy said. "I didn't know that."

"Oh, yes! I went to the circus when I was your age too," Hannah told her. "The clowns were my favorites."

Just then a tiny car stopped in front of them. A lot of clowns started piling out.

"How can they get so many clowns in that car?" George asked.

"They're probably contortionists," Mr. Drew explained. "That means they can bend their bodies into all kinds of shapes, so they can fit anywhere."

"Ow, that hurts me just thinking about it," said Bess.

Next came some clowns riding unicycles. But Nancy noticed something strange. "Where are their noses?" she asked.

"What do you mean?" Bess said.

"All the other clowns have big red balls for noses," Nancy pointed out. "Some of these clowns don't."

"You're right," Bess said. She counted. "Four of them are missing their noses!"

"They look kind of mad, too," George said. "They're not smiling like the other clowns."

After the clowns came the elephants. The woman riding the first one wore a bright pink costume. She was also wearing a huge feather headdress. The woman on the second elephant had on a bright green costume. But she didn't have a feather headdress. Neither did the woman following her.

That's odd, Nancy thought. *Clowns with no noses and elephant riders with no headdresses.*

Behind the elephants, the acrobats were walking and waving to the cheering crowds.

"This is what I've been waiting for," George said. "I love to watch the trapeze acts."

Nancy did too, but she noticed that not all of the trapeze artists were wearing sequined capes. "I wonder if some of their equipment didn't arrive," she said.

"What do you mean?" George asked.

Nancy mentioned the missing noses, head-dresses, and capes. "Why are some of the performers fully dressed but others aren't?" she wondered.

"Are you saying there really is a circus mystery we need to solve?" Bess asked.

Nancy shrugged. "I'm not sure," she said. "But

I think it's kind of strange that so many of the performers are missing parts of their costumes."

"Maybe they just misplaced them," George suggested. "Or maybe they didn't have time to unpack everything after they got off the train."

"You're probably right," Nancy said. "I guess we shouldn't look for mysteries everywhere we go."

For the next two hours Nancy, Bess, and George were thrilled by all the wonderful circus acts.

Then suddenly the lights went out! As the band played a fanfare, a big spotlight went on in the center ring, and Brownie the Bear and his trainer appeared. For several minutes Brownie danced and performed tricks. When the act was over, Brownie and the trainer bowed. The crowd roared its approval. Then the big bear turned away from the trainer and walked over to the front row. He grabbed a lady's purse.

The lady screamed, but the Clue Crew laughed. They knew now that it was part of the

act. When Brownie returned the purse to the lady, the crowd clapped.

"One of these days that bear isn't going to give back what he's taken," Nancy said.

ChaPTER FOUR

The Mystery Boy

"Stop it, Chip!" Bess said. Chocolate Chip, Nancy's chocolate Lab puppy, was trying to push his way inside Bess's sleeping bag. "Leave me alone! I'm still half asleep!" It was Saturday morning, and the girls were waking up in Nancy's room.

George sat up in her sleeping bag and said, "I'm hungry!" She looked over at Nancy, who was stretching, and asked, "Do you think Hannah would fix pancakes for breakfast?"

"You bet!" Nancy told her. She picked up Chocolate Chip and hugged him. "That sounds good to me, too."

Just then the doorbell rang downstairs. A few minutes later, Deirdre pranced into Nancy's bedroom.

"I didn't know you were having a slumber party," Deirdre said. She stuck out her lower lip in a pout. "Why wasn't I invited?"

"It's not a slumber party, Deirdre," Nancy said. "Bess's parents are in Oklahoma, and Mrs. Fayne had to leave early this morning to cater a party in Hailey Town."

"Why are *you* up so early?" Bess asked.

Deirdre's pout became a grin. She held up a handful of papers. "I'm delivering flyers for my circus," she said. She handed one each to Nancy, Bess, and George. "It's going to be so much better than that 'other' circus."

"Deirdre, that 'other' circus is the *real* circus," George said. "Yours is just in your backyard."

"Oh? Well, just you wait and see how 'real' that other circus is," Deirdre said. "You're all in for a big surprise!"

"What is it?" Nancy asked.

"I'm not going to tell," said Deirdre. "You won't even find it on my website until after the first performance."

"That'll be a first," George muttered to Bess.

Deirdre was always posting everyone else's secrets on her website. If you told Deirdre anything, the whole world would know about it in a few hours.

"We saw you at the circus last night," Nancy said, "but then you just disappeared."

"Yeah!" Bess chimed in. "What happened to you?"

"Wouldn't you like to know?" Deirdre said. She gave the three of them another big grin. "Well, I've got to deliver the rest of these flyers. I'll see you tomorrow morning at the 'real' circus."

"Oh, she just makes me so mad sometimes," Bess said.

"Yeah," George agreed. "She thinks she is so cool."

"Deirdre's up to something besides putting on a backyard circus," Nancy said. "Come on, Clue

Crew! We need to get dressed and follow her."

"What about breakfast?" George asked. "I can't solve a mystery on an empty stomach."

"We'll grab energy bars on our way out," Nancy said.

Dressed and with energy bars in hand, Nancy, Bess, and George headed out the front door.

For the next hour the Clue Crew followed Deirdre all over the neighborhood. But they never went more than five blocks in any direction.

Deirdre stopped at the houses of Marcy Rubin, Kendra Jackson, Amanda Johnson, Nadine Nardo, Ned Nickerson, and Peter Patino. They were all in the Clue Crew's class.

"She's just giving them flyers, Nancy," George said. "She's not doing anything else."

"I don't think we're going to solve the mystery this way," added Bess.

Nancy thought for a minute. "She's up to something. I know she is," she said. "We can't give up."

When Deirdre left Peter's house, she turned left at the next corner.

"She's heading home, Nancy," George said.

"This has been a complete bust," complained Bess.

But they continued to follow Deirdre, staying behind big trees lining the edge of the street.

Suddenly, just as Deirdre reached the big wooden fence that marked the edge of her backyard, a side gate opened. A boy with black hair waved her inside. Deirdre gave the boy a big grin, looked around quickly, and then followed him inside.

"Who was that?" Nancy said.

"I don't know, but he was wearing cool shoes," Bess replied.

"I think that boy is a clue. He may have something to do with the surprise Deirdre was telling us about," said Nancy. "We need to get closer."

"There's another gate to the Shannons' backyard off the alley," George reminded the others. "Let's head there."

"Good idea," Nancy said.

The three of them ran toward the alley. When they reached the gate, Nancy opened it slowly. She was glad that Mrs. Shannon liked big shrubs and bushes, because the backyard was full of them. It offered the Clue Crew protection from being seen. They were able to get within a few feet of where Deirdre and the boy were talking.

"Are you sure no one suspects what we're doing?" the boy asked.

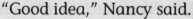

32

"I'm sure," Deirdre said. "What about those three girls you call the Clue Crew?" the boy said.

"Ha!" replied Deirdre. "This mystery is way too hard for them!"

Nancy looked at Bess and George. "We'll show her!" she whispered.

"Good," the boy said.

Just then Deirdre's cell phone rang. She talked softly for a minute, then said, "That was my mother. She's asking me to come inside."

"I'll see you at the circus tonight," the boy said. "We'll finish making our plans." With that, he disappeared through the side gate.

"We'll be there too," Nancy whispered, "and we'll solve this mystery."

CHAPTER FIVE

A Family of Thieves?

When they got to the circus that night, Nancy, Bess, and George wrote their names on the back of their ticket stubs.

Bess blew on hers. "For good luck!" she said.

Nancy and George did the same. Then they dropped them into the big metal box at the entrance to the tent.

Mr. Drew and Hannah put their tickets in too.

"Dad, we want to talk to some of our friends before the circus starts," Nancy said. "Is that all right?"

"As long as you stay in sight," said Mr. Drew.

Nancy could see the circus performers lining

up on the other side of the tent. They were getting ready for the grand entrance. But Nancy thought the Clue Crew had plenty of time to do some sleuthing.

"While we're reminding our friends to put their ticket stubs in the metal box for the drawing, we can also look for Deirdre," she said.

In the section next to theirs, the Clue Crew found Stacy Quinn and her parents. Brianne Slotsky was with them.

"Did you put your ticket stubs in the metal box?" Bess asked.

Stacy and Brianne nodded.

"What a wonderful idea, Nancy," Mrs. Quinn said. "That stuffed bear is huge, and I think the children in the hospital will love it."

"Thanks, Mrs. Quinn," Nancy said. "I just hope we win!"

"Have you seen Deirdre tonight?" asked George.

"We thought we saw her from a distance," Stacy said, "but she was with a boy we'd never seen before, so it could have been somebody else."

"Did the boy have black hair?" Bess asked.

"Yeah!" Brianne said. "How did you know that?"

"Just a guess," Nancy said. She glanced at her watch. "Well, we'll see you later."

As fast as they could, the Clue Crew made their way around the circus tent. They told all their friends not to forget to put their ticket stubs in the metal box for the drawing. They also asked about Deirdre. Everyone had seen her earlier—with a black-haired boy—but no one had seen her since.

"He's kind of cute," Kendra Jackson said. "His hair is almost as pretty as mine."

Kendra was really proud of her shiny black hair.

"I like black and red together," Nadine Nardo said. "His black hair and my red hair would really make people notice us."

Finally Nancy, Bess, and George had made

a complete circle of the tent and were back in their seats. But they weren't any closer to finding Deirdre.

"I have an idea," Bess whispered. "I could disguise my voice and call Deirdre on her cell phone. I could tell her we know what she's doing."

"The Clue Crew doesn't make anonymous telephone calls, Bess," Nancy whispered back. "Anyway, your name comes up when you call people, so she'd know who it was."

"Oh, yeah," Bess said.

"Look!" George said. "There she is!"

Nancy and Bess looked in the direction George was pointing. Deirdre and the boy with black hair were now standing at the entrance where all the circus performers were lining up.

"Why don't they sit in their seats like the rest of us?" Bess said.

Just then the band began to play. The boy with Deirdre pointed to something. Then he leaned over and whispered into Deirdre's ear. Deirdre nodded her head.

"I wish we could hear what they're saying," George said.

"Maybe we need to save our allowance to buy one of those spy microphones," Bess said. She thought for a minute. "Or maybe I could invent something."

Circus music filled the huge tent. As the ring-master led in all the performers, Nancy, Bess, and George watched the parade passing in front of them.

Suddenly Bess said, "Nancy! What happened to their noses?"

"I was wondering the same thing," said Nancy. "Even more of the clowns are missing their noses tonight."

"This can't just be a coincidence, Nancy," George said. "Last night we thought it was because they just hadn't unpacked everything, but—"

"Oh, no!" cried Nancy. "Look!"

Behind the clowns came the elephants. None of the women riding them were wearing their huge feather headdresses.

"All the headdresses are missing tonight too," Nancy said. *"Is somebody stealing them?"*

"Who would want to do something like that?" Bess asked.

A moment later the three girls looked at one

another. "Deirdre!" they said in unison.

"Yes!" George said. "Maybe she's going to use them for her backyard circus!"

"That has to be it!" exclaimed Bess.

"Let me write all this down," Nancy said.

Nancy got out her notebook and pen and wrote, "Circus items are missing. Did Deirdre Shannon steal them? She is putting on a backyard circus. She told us that she had a big surprise. This could be the solution to the mystery!"

By the time the parade was over, Nancy had made a list of the things they thought were missing.

During the performances the Clue Crew watched the acts with one eye and kept the other eye open for Deirdre and the mysterious boy with black hair.

"I still think it's strange that Deirdre isn't watching the circus," Bess whispered. "If she's going to have one in her backyard, she needs to know what the performers do."

"I think I know why she isn't," George said.

"When is the best time to steal all these things?"

"When the performers are performing, that's when!" Nancy replied.

Nancy looked over at Mr. Drew and Hannah. They were laughing about what some of the clowns were doing. "Dad, we need to do some serious detective work," she said. "It can't wait until the circus is over."

"Well, all right, but stay inside the tent where I can see you," Mr. Drew said.

"Okay," Nancy agreed.

The three friends ran down the steps of their section. Then they hurried along the back of the bleachers toward the next section.

"What's up, Nancy?" George asked.

"I just saw Deirdre and that boy pass by the entrance on the other side of the tent," Nancy said. "They were carrying a suitcase."

When the Clue Crew reached the entrance, Nancy said, "Look! That's Deirdre's mother's car!"

Nancy, Bess, and George watched Deirdre get into the backseat with the suitcase. She said something to the black-haired boy. He nodded, then ran off into the darkness, and Mrs. Shannon drove off.

"Deirdre's mother is in on this too!" said Bess. "I can't believe it! It's a family of thieves!"

ChaPTER Six

A New Twist

On Sunday morning Bess and George met at Nancy's, and the three of them pedaled over to Deirdre's house.

"I hear circus music," Bess said.

"Deirdre's flyer said her circus started at ten o'clock," said Nancy. "We still have fifteen minutes."

They leaned their bikes up against a big tree and headed toward Deirdre's backyard. When Nancy opened the gate, Bess let out a gasp.

"Wow! I can't believe this!" cried George. "That tent is huge."

"Deirdre always gets what she wants," Bess said.

The friends went on into the yard. Several of their classmates were milling around outside the tent. They were talking to people dressed like a clown, a horse, a camel, and an elephant.

"Hey! It's the Clue Crew!" Kendra shouted. She ran over to them. "So far this is even better than the real circus. Everything's free—including the peanuts and the cotton candy!"

Nancy looked at Bess and George. "This is bad," she said. "This is really bad."

"Why?" Kendra asked. "You don't have to pay for anything at this circus."

"Exactly!" Nancy said. "If everyone else feels the same way, then they might not go to the real circus, and that means there won't be as many ticket stubs entered for the drawing."

"Oh, yeah! We need as many as possible!" Kendra said. "Well, maybe the acts won't be any good."

"That's not likely," said George. "Everything Deirdre does is top-notch."

"I told Deirdre I could be an ape if she wanted me to," Kendra said. "I still have my ape costume from our school play, but she said she also needed people in the audience, so that's what I'm doing." She looked Nancy, Bess, and George up and down. "That's what you're doing too, isn't it?"

"I'm glad you could tell, Kendra," Bess said. She rolled her eyes.

Just then they heard a loud whistle. The boy with black hair came out of the circus tent. But now he was dressed like a ringmaster.

"What's he doing here?" Nancy whispered.

"That's Joey DeLuca," Kendra said. "He's the son of the ringmaster at the circus."

Nancy, Bess, and George looked at one another.

"So he's Deirdre's surprise," Nancy said.

"Well, one mystery has been solved," said Bess. "We know who that boy is."

"But now we've got another mystery," George said. "Why is he helping Deirdre put on her backyard circus?"

"And don't forget the main mystery," Nancy added. *"Who stole all those things from the real circus?"*

Joey blew his whistle again and cracked a black whip. "Come one! Come all!" he shouted. "Here inside the big top is the Greatest Show on Earth!"

"We need to hurry," Kendra said, "or we won't get very good seats."

Kendra started running toward the entrance to the tent. Nancy, Bess, and George followed right behind her.

When they got inside, Nancy was amazed. There was a ring in the middle of the tent. A trapeze was hanging down above it.

Nancy, Bess, and George took seats with Kendra at the top of the bleachers. Kevin, Madison, Brianne, and Marcy were sitting in the row in front of them.

"Don't forget to go to the other circus tonight," Nancy whispered to them. "We have to win that stuffed bear for the children's hospital."

"We will!" they all promised.

Just then Joey entered and waved to the bleachers. "Welcome to the Greatest Show on Earth!" he shouted. He ran to the center of the ring. "Let the circus begin!"

On cue, Deirdre pranced in. She was wearing a pink ballerina costume. She was holding

Marshmallow, her white cat. Behind Deirdre marched Peter. He had on purple tights and an orange cape. Nancy thought he looked really embarrassed.

"Love the color!" Kevin shouted.

The clown, the horse, the camel, and the elephant followed Peter.

When everyone was inside the tent, Joey cracked his whip and shouted, "Our first act will be Miss Deirdre and her rare but dangerous white tiger!" He put two kitchen stools a few inches apart in the center of the ring.

With Marshmallow in her arms, Deirdre ran into the ring. She pranced around for a couple of minutes, then put the cat on one of the stools. She held a ring between the two stools, and Marshmallow jumped through it onto the other stool.

The crowd cheered.

"Well, I take back all the unkind things I ever said about that cat," George said. "That wasn't bad."

After Deirdre, Peter swung by his legs from the trapeze, the clown acted silly, and the horse, the camel, and the elephant each did a couple of tricks.

"Well, that's the show, folks," Joey said finally. "We hope you enjoyed it."

The crowd roared.

"I didn't see any of those things that are

missing from the circus," George said. "I guess Deirdre and Joey didn't take them after all."

"Well, we don't know that for sure, George," Nancy said. "We only know that they didn't use them in the circus."

"Good point, Nancy," said Bess. "It's still a mystery what happened to them."

The three friends joined the rest of the crowd in the center of the ring, where everyone was congratulating the circus performers.

Deirdre introduced Nancy, Bess, and George to Joey.

"You're a great ringmaster," George told him. "Are you going to follow in your father's footsteps when he retires?"

"Not me! I hate the circus. We travel all the time and I never get to stay in one place long enough to make good friends," Joey said. "I'd love to live right here in River Heights and have a normal life."

Nancy though Joey sounded sad. "And I have a plan to make that happen, too," he added.

ChAPTER SEVEN

Dead End?

When Joey turned around to say something to Deirdre, Bess whispered, "We may have our thief after all!"

"What do you mean?" George asked.

"Well, Joey said he wants to lead a normal life," Bess explained, "so maybe he's trying to close down the circus by stealing the costumes."

"I don't know, Bess," said Nancy. "Wouldn't it take a really long time to do that?"

Bess thought for a minute. "Joey might not plan to steal them all," she said. "He could steal just enough that some of the performers would get mad and quit."

"Or people would stop going to see the

circus," George said. "It's not much of a circus if the clowns are only wearing their street clothes!"

"Hmm," Nancy said. "This is kind of beginning to make sense. Joey!" she called.

Joey turned back around. "Yeah?" he said.

"Would you be able to give us a backstage tour before the show tonight?" Nancy asked. "We'd like to see what goes on behind the scenes."

"Sure. No problem!" Joey replied. "I'll meet you at the main entrance."

"Cool!" Nancy said. "We'll be there."

Just then Brianne and Madison asked Joey to sign their autograph books.

"Now that I think about it, he doesn't act like somebody who's been stealing costumes, Nancy," Bess whispered. "I wouldn't want a lot of people snooping around if I were guilty."

"That's just it, Bess," Nancy said. "Dad told me that some criminals try to make you think that they're being cooperative. But they really just want to make sure you don't find anything that might make you suspicious of them."

"If he's the thief, then maybe we'll find where he's hidden everything," George said.

"We should be so lucky," Bess said.

"Well, I promised Hannah I'd help her clean out the cupboards in the kitchen before we go to the circus tonight, so I need to go home," Nancy said.

The three friends jumped on their bicycles and left Deirdre's house.

That evening Bess and George arrived at Nancy's in time to have some of Hannah's freshly baked cookies before they headed to the circus. But Hannah had a headache and decided to stay home.

In the car on the way to the show, Nancy said, "Daddy, Joey DeLuca is going to give us a behind-the-scenes tour before tonight's performance. He's the ringmaster's son, but we think he may be the one who's stealing parts of everyone's costumes. That way, the circus will close and he can live a normal life here in River Heights."

"That's an odd way of trying to put the circus out of business," Mr. Drew commented.

"That's what I thought too, Daddy," Nancy said.

"But criminals do odd things sometimes," said Mr. Drew. "Just make sure you three stay together while you're sleuthing."

"Oh, we will," Nancy assured him. "We never do anything foolish."

"All right," Mr. Drew said. "I'll probably look around the area myself. I've always wanted to see what went on behind the scenes." He looked over at Nancy and grinned. "But I'll stay out of sight so I won't embarrass you."

"You won't embarrass us, Daddy," Nancy said. "You're one of our top investigators."

When they got to the circus, Mr. Drew parked the car. He followed Nancy, Bess, and George as they headed toward the main entrance. In a few minutes Joey appeared, still dressed in his ringmaster outfit.

Nancy introduced him to Mr. Drew. Then Joey asked, "Are you ready?"

"We sure are!" the three friends cried.

With Joey in the lead, they started walking to the back of the huge tent. Some of the performers were coming out of their trailers, heading toward the circus tent.

"We'll be able to see more after everyone's gone," Joey said. "That's when I really like wandering around out here."

"I bet," George muttered. "You can take whatever you want."

Nancy nudged her to keep quiet.

"Do you collect anything?" Bess asked. "You know, like *circus* souvenirs?"

Joey gave her a puzzled look. "Like what?" he said.

"Like clown noses or acrobat capes or feather headdresses," Nancy said.

Joey winkled his nose. "Are you serious?" he

said. "Why would I want to do that? I'm trying to forget the circus, not remember it."

The three friends looked at one another.

"But it's funny that you ask, because some-body must," Joey continued. "A lot of those things you just mentioned have turned up missing." He stopped and looked at them. "Hey, wait a minute! You three are the Clue Crew! You go around solving mysteries, don't you?" He gave them a knowing look. "You thought I was the one taking all those things, didn't you?"

"Well, you said you had a plan to stay in River Heights," Nancy explained, "and we thought maybe if you closed down the circus, you could do that."

Suddenly, Bess screamed.

Nancy, George, and Joey turned.

Brownie the Bear was heading right toward them! And he didn't look very happy.

CHAPTER EIGHT

A Really Great Trick!

"You don't have to be afraid of Brownie," Joey reassured them. "He won't hurt you."

"What's he doing loose?" Nancy asked.

"That's one of Brownie's tricks," Joey explained. "He can unlock his cage."

"Are you serious?" George said.

Joey nodded. "We usually just let him stay out for a while," he said. "He doesn't really do anything except wander around."

Bess clutched her purse tightly. "He's not getting this!" she declared. "It's the only one I have that goes with my outfit!"

"Letting a bear walk around loose sounds kind of dangerous," Nancy said.

Joey shrugged. "That's circus life for you," he said.

Right at that moment, Brownie's trainer came running around the corner. He stopped when he saw Joey and the Clue Crew. "Sorry," he said. He attached a leash to Brownie and led him gently back to his cage.

Nancy was impressed by how well he treated the bear.

"I think it's really neat that you want to stay in River Heights and go to school with us," she told Joey. "You said you had a plan to make it happen. What is it?"

"Well, I guess it's really not much of a plan," he said, "but my dad knows that I don't want to be in the circus when I grow up, so I'm always talking to him about how important it is that I go to a real school."

"River Heights Elementary is a great school," Bess said. "We just won a national award."

"I know. My uncle Frank told me. He lives here in River Heights," Joey said. He grinned.

"I could stay with him and his family."

"Super!" George said.

"Helping Deirdre put on her backyard circus was also part of my plan," Joey said. "I heard her asking some of the performers for advice on how to do it, so I thought if I could show Dad how well I got along with the kids here, he might think about letting me stay."

"What if your plan doesn't work?" Bess asked.

Joey shrugged. "Then I'll just stay with the circus," he said.

In the distance Nancy heard the band starting to play.

"We'd better take our seats," Nancy said. "Thanks for the tour, Joey."

"You're welcome," Joey said. "Enjoy the show!"

Nancy saw Mr. Drew standing a few yards away. She waved. Mr. Drew waved back.

When the Clue Crew reached him, Nancy frowned. "Well, we struck out again, Dad. Joey DeLuca isn't the one who's been stealing parts of the costumes. We're back where we started," she said.

"That can happen when you're trying to solve a crime, girls," Mr. Drew said. "It's two steps forward, three steps backward sometimes. But if you don't give up, you'll eventually solve the case."

"Oh, we don't plan to give up, Mr. Drew," George said.

"The Clue Crew never gives up!" Bess added.

By the time they found their seats, the circus parade had already started. Nancy, Bess, and George all noticed that there were even more things missing now. None of the clowns had their big red noses. And none of the acrobats had their sequined capes. And Nancy noticed that now some of the jugglers were even missing their bowling pins!

"They all look like they're really angry," Nancy said.

Just then two white horses pulled a big red and white cage in front of their section and stopped. Brownie was inside. He was dressed for his performance, in a red hat and a red vest.

Brownie's trainer ran to the center of the ring. He stood there for a few minutes.

"What's he waiting for?" a man in front of Nancy asked the woman next to him.

"Well, what are you waiting for?" the trainer shouted toward the cage. "The good people here are expecting us to put on a show."

At that, Brownie lay on his back and started pedaling his legs. The crowd laughed.

"If you don't work, you don't get paid," the trainer shouted to Brownie.

Brownie sat up quickly and opened his mouth in a grin. That made the audience applaud.

Then Brownie reached over, unlatched his cage, stepped out, and started walking toward the trainer.

At first the crowd gasped. Then they applauded again.

"Can that bear actually let himself out of his cage?" Mr. Drew asked.

"You bet!" Nancy said. "Joey said he even walks around the circus grounds by himself sometimes."

"Well, I'm not quite sure that's smart," Mr. Drew said. "He may be trained, but he's still a wild animal, and they can just as suddenly—"

Before Mr. Drew could finish his sentence, Brownie stopped, turned away from the trainer, and raced to the front row, where he grabbed a lady's purse.

Several people screamed. Then the crowd laughed, as Brownie handed the purse back to the lady.

Nancy turned to Bess and George. "I have an idea," she said.

ChaPTER NiNE

The Mystery Is Solved!

As soon as the last act was over, Nancy said, "Daddy, I think we can solve this case tonight, but we need to talk to Joey again."

"Well, they're about to have the drawing for the stuffed bear, Nancy," Mr. Drew said. "And remember that you have to be here when your name is called in order to win."

The Clue Crew looked at one another.

"It's a tough choice," Nancy said, "but the children in the hospital come before our solving mysteries."

Bess and George nodded.

A trumpet sounded, and a spotlight shone on the ringmaster in the center ring. A clown carried the metal box to him. The ringmaster opened the box and drew out a name.

"And the winner is . . . Hannah Gruen!" the ringmaster shouted.

"Oh, no!" cried Nancy. "You have to be here to win!"

"Here I am!"

Just then the Clue Crew saw Hannah running toward the center ring. She grabbed the microphone. "I had a headache, so I stayed home. But just a few minutes ago I realized that I couldn't let Nancy Drew and the Clue Crew down, just in case I won. So I got into my car and drove here. The children in the hospital are more important than my headache!"

"Way to go, Hannah!" the Clue Crew shouted.

The spotlight found them, and they waved to the cheering crowd.

"I think you can go solve the mystery now," Mr. Drew whispered to Nancy. "Hannah and I will take care of the stuffed bear for you and meet you at the car in fifteen minutes."

"Thanks, Daddy!" Nancy said.

"But it's already dark, so just make sure you stay under the lights and around people," Mr. Drew added.

"You got it!" Bess and George said.

"Come on!" Nancy said. "There's Joey!"

The three friends raced down the steps of their section and across the center ring to the other side of the tent.

"Joey!" Nancy called. "Wait up!"

Joey turned. "Oh, hi," he said. "Congratulations. I'm happy that you won the stuffed bear."

"You don't act very happy," Bess said.

Joey let out a big sigh. "Dad won't let me stay in River Heights," he told them. "He's really angry that somebody has been stealing things from the performers, and he doesn't want to talk about anything else." He sighed again. "I guess I'll never have a normal life."

"Well, maybe we can do something about that," Nancy said. She looked at Bess and George. "Can't we, Clue Crew?"

Bess and George nodded. "You bet!" they answered.

Joey shook his head. "I know you three have solved a lot of mysteries here in River Heights," he said, "but I'm sure this is bigger than the kind of cases you've worked on."

"Hey! You take that back!" Bess said. She was standing with her hands on her hips. "A crime is a crime is a crime! Those were just as important to the people they happened to as yours is."

"I'm sorry," Joey said. "I didn't mean to—"

"It's all right," said George. "We know you're upset."

"So how can you help me solve my problem?" Joey said.

"Where's Brownie?" Nancy asked.

"He's probably already in his cage, ready for the parade to the circus train," Joey replied. "Why?"

"Is it the same cage he was in during the performance?" Nancy asked.

Joey shook his head. "No, his real cage is

bigger," he said. "It's the one he stays in when we're traveling."

"Can we see it?" George asked.

"All right," Joey said.

When they reached Brownie's cage, the trainer was standing beside it.

"Harry, these are some friends of mine who live here in River Heights," Joey said. "They wanted to see Brownie one more time before we left."

Nancy thought Harry looked mad about something. Brownie was sitting inside his cage, but he had his back turned to everyone.

"We really do like

Brownie," Nancy said. "He does some great tricks."

"He sure does," Bess and George agreed.

"Well, there's one trick I'm going to have to *un*teach him," Harry said. "Opening the door of his cage."

Brownie opened his mouth and made a noise. Nancy was

almost positive that it sounded like a giggle.

"Why don't you just put a padlock on it?" George suggested.

"I tried that, but it makes him unhappy," Harry explained, "and he won't perform his tricks if he's unhappy."

Nancy was looking at the rear of the cage. She pointed to a huge pile of blankets. "What are those for?" she asked.

"That's Brownie's bed," Harry replied.

"It looks kind of lumpy to me," said Bess. "I'd never be able to sleep on that."

Harry shrugged. "Well, it doesn't seem to bother Brownie," he said. "Look, kids, I'd love to stand here and talk to you some more, but—"

"Could we look underneath the blankets?" Nancy interrupted.

Harry gave them a puzzled look. "What for?" he asked.

"We're trying to solve a mystery," Bess told him. "We look everywhere for evidence."

"Well, you're not going to find any *evidence*

here," Harry said, "but I don't have time to argue."

Harry opened the cage. He climbed inside and headed toward the blankets. Brownie made his giggling noise again. Nancy, George, and Bess just looked at one another.

When Harry lifted the pile, everyone gasped. Underneath were the clowns' big red noses, the sequined capes, the feather headdresses, and several bowling pins.

"Brownie's the circus thief!" Nancy declared.

Chapter Ten

Circus Stars!

"Look, everybody!" Joey called out to the circus performers. "The thief was Brownie!"

Several of the clowns ran over to Brownie's cage. "Joey's right!" they shouted. "Here are our missing noses."

The clowns got their big red noses. The acrobats got their sequined capes. The women who rode the elephants got their feather headdresses. And the jugglers got their bowling pins.

Finally, everything that Brownie had stolen had been returned.

"Dad! Dad!" Joey shouted. "The Clue Crew solved the mystery!"

Mr. DeLuca came up and put his arm around

Joey. He was still dressed in his ringmaster's outfit. "I'd like to meet the detectives who saved my circus," he said.

Joey introduced Nancy, Bess, and George to his father. "They've solved a lot of other mysteries here in River Heights too," he said. "They're famous."

"We all thought it was one of the performers," Mr. DeLuca said. "That was bad for morale. Everyone was suspicious of everyone else. We had some performers who were going to quit and go to another circus."

"It would be great to go to school with friends like the Clue Crew," Joey said.

Mr. DeLuca looked down at Joey. "I've been thinking about what you said, son, and if you really want to stay in River Heights with Uncle Frank, then I'm going to let you."

"Oh, Dad!" Joey exclaimed. "That's great! Thank you so much!"

"There's one condition, though," Mr. DeLuca added. "You have to spend some time during the summer with the circus, because I'll really miss you."

"It's a deal, Dad!" Joey agreed.

Just then Mr. Drew walked up. Nancy introduced him to everyone.

Mr. DeLuca turned to the Clue Crew. "You deserve a reward for solving this mystery," he said. He pulled out his wallet. "I think that—"

"We don't want any money, Mr. DeLuca," Nancy told him, "but there is something else."

"You name it!" Mr. DeLuca said.

"Could we ride on one of the elephants for the trip back to the circus train?" Nancy said.

"Oh, wow!" Bess and George exclaimed. "That would be so cool."

Mr. DeLuca looked at Mr. Drew. "Well, I think that can be arranged, if it's all right with Mr. Drew," he said.

"I don't see why not," Mr. Drew said. "And I think I can speak for Bess's and George's parents too."

"Tina!" shouted Mr. DeLuca.

One of the elephant riders ran over to where they were all standing. "Yes, Mr. DeLuca," she said.

"Would you find some costumes for these girls?" the ringmaster said. "They're going to ride Julie to the train."

"Of course! I'll do anything for the Clue Crew," Tina said. "They got my favorite feather headdress back for me."

The Clue Crew followed Tina to her trailer. She found perfect costumes for all three of them. When they were dressed, Tina took them to where the elephants were already lined up.

"Tony! Julie has some riders after all!" Tina called. "The Clue Crew!"

"Great!" Tony exclaimed. He set a ladder next to Julie, and the Clue Crew climbed up and onto the elephant's back. "I'll be leading her, so you won't have to do anything except wave to the crowd," Tony told them. He climbed up the ladder and helped the girls strap themselves into Julie's safety harness.

"We can do that!" the three friends said.

A few minutes later Tony said, "Here we go, Clue Crew!" He held out his elephant hook, and Julie grabbed it with her trunk.

"Oh!" Bess cried. "Won't that point hurt her?"

"No," Nancy assured her. "It's just used for commands, and elephants know that."

Within minutes they had left the circus grounds and were headed through downtown River Heights.

The crowds waved and cheered when they saw Nancy, Bess, and George. Several of their friends shouted, "Clue Crew! Clue Crew!"

The Clue Crew waved back.

"This is so cool!" Bess said. "I feel like I'm really in the circus."

Suddenly the girls saw Deirdre. She was standing with Madison and Amanda.

"How did you get to do that?" Deirdre shouted to them. "It should have been me! I'm the one with the backyard circus!"

"We solved the mystery!" Nancy called back.

"We found the circus thief!"

"Who was it?" Madison yelled.

Just then the Clue Crew heard a scream from behind them. They turned. Brownie had reached out of his cage and grabbed a woman's purse. Harry was scolding him and telling him to return it. Reluctantly the bear handed the woman back her purse. The crowd laughed.

"One guess!" George shouted to Madison.

Ahead they could see the circus train at the station.

"I don't want the parade to end," Bess said. "I think I'm really good at this!"

"I know something else we're really good at," Nancy said. "Solving mysteries." She grinned. "I wonder what the next one will be?"

Have Your Picture Taken with Brownie the Bear at the Circus!

Now that you've gone to the circus with Nancy and the Clue Crew, you can have your picture taken with Brownie the Bear.

You Will Need:

An inexpensive 8 x 10 picture frame (with glass or clear plastic)

Rounded-point scissors

Glue

8 x 10 construction paper (one sheet each of white, brown, and black)

A big glass, a small glass, a large button, and a small button

A black crayon or marker

A picture of yourself that your parents will let you cut out

❀ Put the mouth of the big glass on the brown construction paper and draw around the rim to make Brownie's head.

❀ Put the mouth of the small glass on the brown construction paper and draw around the rim to make his snout (the nose and mouth).

❀ Put the large button on the brown construction paper and draw around the edge to make Brownie's two ears. Cut out the circles and set them aside.

❀ Put the large button on top of the black construction paper and draw around the rim to make Brownie's nose.

❀ Put the small button on top of the black construction paper and draw around the edge to make his two eyes. Cut out the circles and set them aside.

❀Place the head circle and the snout circle in the lower right-hand side of the white construction paper, about an inch from the bottom and a half inch from the right side. Let the bottom circle overlap the top circle. Glue these two circles onto the white construction paper.

❀ Next, take the two brown ears and glue them at angles to the head circle.

❀ Draw a smile (with the black crayon or marker) on the top brown circle.

❀ Then glue the black nose just above it.

❀ Finally, glue the two black eyes onto the head.

Now you have Brownie the Bear! But you need to put yourself beside him.

Here's what to do:

❀ Take the picture your parents let you have and cut around yourself.

❀ Glue yourself next to Brownie.

❀ If you want, you can draw in the background where you had this picture taken: under some trees, in front of the circus tent, or in front of Brownie's cage. It's up to you!

*When you've finished, put the picture in the frame and hang it on your wall. You'll be able to show all your friends that you had your picture taken with Brownie after you read *Circus Scare*. They also may want to read it and then have their picture taken with Brownie the Bear!

Goddess Girls

✴ READ ABOUT ALL YOUR FAVORITE GODDESSES!

#1 ATHENA THE BRAIN

#2 PERSEPHONE THE PHONY

#3 APHRODITE THE BEAUTY

#4 ARTEMIS THE BRAVE

From Aladdin

PUBLISHED BY SIMON & SCHUSTER

HUNGRY FOR MORE MAD SCIENCE?

CATCH UP WITH FRANNY AS SHE CONDUCTS OTHER EXPERIMENTS!

THIRD-GRADE DETECTIVES

Everyone in the third grade loves the new teacher, Mr. Merlin.
Mr. Merlin used to be a spy, and he knows all about secret codes and the strange and gross ways the police solve mysteries.

You can help decode the clues and solve the mystery in these other stories about the Third-Grade Detectives:

ALADDIN PAPERBACKS • Simon & Schuster Children's Publishing • www.SimonSaysKids.

Ready-for-Chapters